S0-CAP-041

WITHDRAWN

*Dear Parent:*

## *Your child's love of reading starts here!*

Every child learns to read in a different way and at his or her own speed. Some go back and forth between reading levels and read favorite books again and again. Others read through each level in order. You can help your young reader improve and become more confident by encouraging his or her own interests and abilities. From books your child reads with you to the first books he or she reads alone, there are I Can Read Books for every stage of reading:

### SHARED READING
Basic language, word repetition, and whimsical illustrations, ideal for sharing with your emergent reader

### BEGINNING READING
Short sentences, familiar words, and simple concepts for children eager to read on their own

### READING WITH HELP
Engaging stories, longer sentences, and language play for developing readers

### READING ALONE
Complex plots, challenging vocabulary, and high-interest topics for the independent reader

**I Can Read Books** have introduced children to the joy of reading since 1957. Featuring award-winning authors and illustrators and a fabulous cast of beloved characters, I Can Read Books set the standard for beginning readers.

A lifetime of discovery begins with the magical words **"I Can Read!"**

*Visit www.icanread.com for information*
*on enriching your child's reading experience.*

*To Mom and Dad,*
*who always allowed me to*
*be the person I wanted to be.*
*—M.I.*

I Can Read® and I Can Read Book® are trademarks of HarperCollins Publishers.

Gigi and Ojiji: Food for Thought
Copyright © 2023 by Melissa Iwai
All rights reserved. Printed in the United States of America.
No part of this book may be used or reproduced in any manner whatsoever without written permission except in the case of brief quotations embodied in critical articles and reviews. For information address HarperCollins Children's Books, a division of HarperCollins Publishers, 195 Broadway, New York, NY 10007.
www.icanread.com

Library of Congress Control Number: 2023932461
ISBN 978-0-06-320812-4 (trade bdg.)—ISBN 978-0-06-320811-7 (pbk.)

Book design by Stephanie Hays
23 24 25 26 27  LB  10 9 8 7 6 5 4 3 2 1     First Edition

# GIGI AND OJIJI

## FOOD FOR THOUGHT

### MELISSA IWAI

**HARPER**
*An Imprint of HarperCollinsPublishers*

"Good morning!" said Gigi.

"Good morning!" said Dad.

"You're up very early," said Mom.

"I'm making breakfast today," said Gigi.

"That's very grown up of you," said Mom.

"I'm impressed!"

"What are you going to make?" Dad asked.

"It's a surprise," said Gigi.

Gigi had bread, peanut butter,

bananas, and berries.

Gigi's Japanese grandpa, Ojiji, came in.

"Ohayo!" he said.

That means good morning in Japanese.

"I made peanut butter toast!" said Gigi.

"Oh!" said Ojiji.

"It's my favorite breakfast!" said Gigi.

"Arigatoo!" he said.

Gigi knew that meant thank you.

Gigi took a big bite of toast.

"Yummy," said Mom.

"Do you like it, Ojiji?" asked Gigi.

"Oishii . . ." said Ojiji.

"It tastes good," he said.

Gigi knew oishii meant delicious.

After breakfast, Gigi helped clear the table.
"Hey . . ." she said,
"Ojiji didn't eat all his food!"

"Maybe he wasn't very hungry," said Mom.

"He hated my breakfast!" Gigi said.

"No, Gigi, I don't think so," said Mom.

"I don't think he likes peanut butter."

"What?!" said Gigi.

"How can anyone NOT like peanut butter?!"

Gigi loved peanut butter.

Everyone she knew did too.

Even Roscoe!

"It's not a common food in Japan," Mom said.

"Ojiji's probably just not used to it."

Gigi tried to understand.

"What do people eat for breakfast

in Japan?" she asked.

"Can we make that for Ojiji tomorrow?"

The next day, Mom made a Japanese breakfast.

"This looks like dinner!" said Gigi.

"Oishii!" said Ojiji.

Gigi saw that Mom and Ojiji

had one more bowl each.

She and Dad didn't have that extra dish.

PICKLES

SALMON

?

RICE

MISO
SOUP

"What's that?" asked Gigi.

"It's natto," said Ojiji.

"They're soybeans," said Mom.

"Do you want to try some?"

Gigi wasn't sure.

The natto smelled funny.

It was sticky and slimy.

"You don't have to," said Ojiji.

"I hated it when I was small.

But I love it now."

Gigi took a bite.

It tasted like it smelled!

Gigi swallowed.

"Oishii . . ." she said.

"Wow!" said Mom.

"Amazing!" said Dad.

"Erai!—Great!" said Ojiji.

"You're better than I was at your age!"

That night, Mom made veggie pancakes.

Gigi loved when her mom made them.

"Surprise!" Mom said.

"I put natto in them!"

"Oishii!" said Ojiji.

"Delicious!" said Dad.

"Uh-oh," thought Gigi.

She took a small bite.

The natto wasn't as stinky
and slimy as before.
But it still tasted funny.
Gigi had an idea.
She hid the natto in her napkin.

"Oh no!" said Gigi.

"Gigi!" said Mom.

"I'm sorry," said Gigi.

"If you didn't like it," said Dad,

"why didn't you just say so?"

"It's okay, Gigi," Ojiji said.
"You don't have to like everything,
even if other people love it.
The important thing is you tried it."

"But you said I was erai," said Gigi.

"You ARE great!" said Ojiji.

"You were brave.

You tried the natto!" he said.

"Maybe when you're older you'll like it."

"Maybe when you're older," said Gigi,

"you'll like peanut butter, Ojiji!"

"Yes," he said, laughing.

"Maybe I will!"

"Look!" said Gigi.

There was someone in the family

who loved both!

# GLOSSARY

**Arigatoo** Thank you

**Erai** Great or excellent

**Natto** Fermented soybeans

**Ohayo** Good morning

**Oishii** Delicious

31901069594705